WILDLIFE AROUND US

REPTILES, AMPHIBIANS & INSECTS: FIELD GUIDE & DRAWING BOOK

Learn how to identify and draw reptiles, amphibians, and insects from the great outdoors!

This library edition published in 2019 by Walter Foster Jr.,
an imprint of The Quarto Group
26391 Crown Valley Parkway, Suite 220, Mission Viejo, CA 92691, USA.
© 2017 Quarto Publishing Group USA Inc.
Published by Walter Foster Jr.,
an imprint of The Quarto Group
All rights reserved. Walter Foster Jr. is trademarked.

The National Wildlife Federation & Ranger Rick contributors:
Children's Publication Staff, Licensing Staff, and in-house naturalist David Mizejewski.

© National Wildlife Federation. All rights reserved.
www.RangerRick.com

Photos © Shutterstock, except yellow jacket phot on page 31 © Franco Folini.
Illustrations by Diana Fisher.

All rights reserved. No part of this book may be reproduced in any form without written permission of the copyright owners. All images in this book have been reproduced with the knowledge and prior consent of the artists concerned, and no responsibility is accepted by producer, publisher, or printer for any infringement of copyright or otherwise, arising from the contents of this publication. Every effort has been made to ensure that credits accurately comply with information supplied. We apologize for any inaccuracies that may have occurred and will resolve inaccurate or missing information in a subsequent reprinting of the book.

Distributed in the United States and Canada by
Lerner Publisher Services
241 First Avenue North
Minneapolis, MN 55401 U.S.A.
www.lernerbooks.com

First Library Edition

Library of Congress Cataloging-in-Publication Data

Names: Walter Foster Jr. (Firm), publisher.
Title: Reptiles, amphibians & insects : field guide & drawing book : learn how to identify and draw reptiles, amphibians & insects from the great outdoors!
Description: First library edition. | Mission Viejo, CA : Walter Foster Jr., an imprint of The Quarto Group, 2019. | Series: Ranger Rick's wildlife around us | Audience: Age 8+ | Audience: Grade 4 to 6.
Identifiers: LCCN 2018051335 | ISBN 9781942875840 (hardcover)
Subjects: LCSH: Reptiles--North America--Juvenile literature. | Amphibians--North America--Juvenile literature. | Insects--North America--Juvenile literature.
Classification: LCC QL644.2 .R48 2019 | DDC 597.9--dc23 LC record available at https://lccn.loc.gov/2018051335

Printed in USA
1 3 5 7 9 10 8 6 4 2

TABLE OF CONTENTS

GETTING STARTED 4

Naturalist Fieldwork 5

Sketching & Coloring Animals 6

Your Naturalist Notebook 7

FASCINATING REPTILES & AMPHIBIANS 8

Identifying Reptiles & Amphibians 10

Common Box Turtle 12

Alligator 14

Pacific Tree Frog 16

Red Salamander 18

INCREDIBLE INSECTS 20

Identifying Insects 22

Monarch Butterfly 24

Cricket 26

Walking Stick 28

Yellow Jacket 30

Continue the Adventure! 32

Welcome to Ranger Rick's field guide to North American critters! Join us as you learn about the reptiles, amphibians, and insects that surround you, from the Pacific tree frog to the monarch butterfly. This book contains step-by-step drawing projects to help you bring each featured animal to life. You'll also find fieldwork tips, fascinating animal facts, and colorful photographs throughout to inspire you in your quest for knowledge. Enjoy the journey!

GETTING STARTED

In this chapter, you'll learn how to prepare for outdoor excursions—from packing your backpack and taking great photos to recording notes and drawings.

When we're busy at school and in our homes, it can be hard to remember that people are part of nature! We are animals, too—and we're an important part of the circle of life. Unlike other animals, we have the unique ability to study and protect other species. The first step in accomplishing this is to get outside and learn about nature. Let's start NOW!

Why spend time outdoors?

You'll get smarter.
The world around you is fascinating, with living organisms everywhere you look! The more time you spend outdoors, the more you'll notice, be curious, and learn.

You'll help animals.
The more you learn about the animals that surround us, the more likely you'll be to protect them. Human decisions can have a big impact on the natural environment, so you will use your new knowledge to conserve threatened animals and the plants they need to thrive.

You'll be healthier.
Fresh air, sun, and exercise make exploring the outdoors great for your body. It improves distance vision too! Spending time in nature is also proven to calm your mind and lift your spirits.

NATURALIST FIELDWORK

A *naturalist* is someone who studies natural life, like plants and animals. And *fieldwork* is what people do when they go out into the real world, into nature, to study, rather than learning in a classroom or lab. Once you get outside and start observing nature, you will be a naturalist doing fieldwork! Naturalists who go into the field prepared are the ones who do the best work and have the most fun.

Go with:

A research assistant. Your assistant is there to help you observe and record, and also for safety. If you venture outside of your backyard, make sure your assistant is an adult.

Wear:

- Hat
- Sunscreen
- Socks and comfortable, sturdy shoes
- Appropriate clothing for the weather

Bring:

A backpack with the following:

- Bottle of water
- Pencil
- Notebook for sketching and taking notes
- Magnifying glass (for viewing small critters)
- Binoculars
- Camera
- Map or GPS device and compass, or a smartphone with these functionalities

Be:

1. **Quiet and still.** You can't observe critters if you've scared them away!
2. **At a distance.** You don't want to hurt any animals or get hurt yourself! You could get bitten or stung, so keep a safe distance.
3. **Patient.** The longer you watch, the more you'll learn. It can take a long time to spot a creature, so practice patience.

SKETCHING & COLORING ANIMALS

To draw the animals in this book, you'll need a few art supplies: paper or a sketchbook, a pencil, an eraser, and a pencil sharpener. Then find some coloring tools, such as crayons, colored pencils, or markers. You'll need an array of bright, beautiful colors for the animals in this book!

Many naturalists are also artists! They spend time observing and recording all the visual details of their subjects. Many of them use paint, such as watercolor, to add color to their work. Watercolor is one of the easiest paints to use—you can clean it up with soap and water! Tempera and acrylic are good non-toxic options, too.

The step-by-step instructions in this book start with basic shapes, such as circles, triangles, and rectangles. Follow the steps in order, copying the new lines in each step and erasing when necessary. Before you know it, you'll have a complete sketch to color! You can use colored pencils, crayons, markers, or even paints to bring these animals to life.

Pencil **Colored pencil** **Crayon** **Marker**

YOUR NATURALIST NOTEBOOK

Now that you're all packed and ready to do some fieldwork, know that there's no right or wrong way to fill up your naturalist notebook. Just observe and record!

Pacific Green Tree Frog
- Type: Amphibian
- Season seen: Spring
- Date seen: May 3
- Size: About 1.5" long

Brown stripe across its eye

Some brown markings

Found Pacific green tree frog while on a family hike in Oregon.

Light green with a pale stomach

Sticky pads on its toes allowed it to stock to the side of a big leaf.

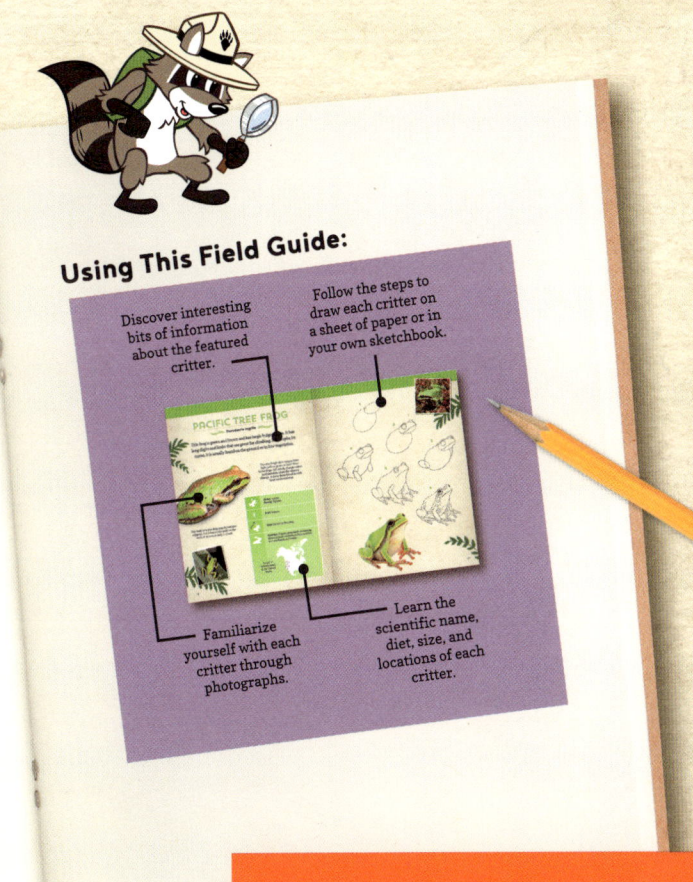

Using This Field Guide:

Discover interesting bits of information about the featured critter.

Follow the steps to draw each critter on a sheet of paper or in your own sketchbook.

Familiarize yourself with each critter through photographs.

Learn the scientific name, diet, size, and locations of each critter.

See a critter on a wall or on the ground? Watch it and record everything you see. What does it look like? What is its main color? Are there any other colors? How big is it? What is its shape like?

What is the critter doing? Is it eating something? How does it move around?

For more color, you can add photos of each critter to your notebook's pages!

Many new species are discovered every year—and about half of all newly discovered species are insects. Maybe you could find something new while doing fieldwork!

So get outside, look for critters, and have fun!

FASCINATING REPTILES & AMPHIBIANS

Herpetology is the study of reptiles and amphibians. When you're watching and recording information about these creatures, you are a naturalist and a herpetologist in training!

The green anole is a lizard and a reptile.

This amphibian is called a red eft, the juvenile phase of the red spotted newt.

Although reptiles and amphibians are cold-blooded animals that are often grouped together, they have some very important differences. At right, see which animals are reptiles and which are amphibians. Then learn about their main differences on the next page!

Reptiles	Amphibians
snakes	frogs
lizards	toads
turtles	salamanders
tortoises	newts
crocodiles	
alligators	

Reptiles vs. Amphibians

How are they born?
Most reptiles lay their eggs on dry land, but some give birth to live young. Reptile hatchlings emerge from the shells as miniature versions of the adults. Most amphibians, however, lay their eggs in water or moist areas on land in large clumps that resemble jelly. In most species, the eggs hatch into tadpoles or larvae that look nothing like adults, and must go through drastic changes, called metamorphosis, into their adult forms.

How do they breathe?
Reptiles breathe through a pair of lungs. Amphibians, however, are born with gills. As they undergo metamorphosis, most amphibians develop lungs. But that's not all! Oxygen can also pass through an amphibian's skin. This process is called "cutaneous respiration." Some amphibians never develop lungs at all, relying solely on their skin to breathe!

Where do they live?
Reptiles have thick, scaly skin that allows some species to live in dry environments. The skin of most amphibians, however, is slippery and moist. These creatures must live in water or damp environments. Because reptiles and amphibians are cold-blooded, they are less active and harder to find in cold temperatures.

Watch out!
In North America, some reptiles you might encounter are venomous. Keep your distance from these animals, just in case!

American Green Tree Frog

IDENTIFYING REPTILES & AMPHIBIANS

Size

Can you guess the size of the animal in inches or feet? If not, compare it to an animal you know well. Is it bigger than a rabbit? Smaller than a mouse?

Shape

What is the animal's overall shape? Does it have a long body or long limbs? Is there any part of the animal that stands out, such as bulging eyes or a small head?

Color

What is the animal's main color? What other colors and patterns are present?

Desert Tortoise
Size & Shape: About 1 foot long with a domed shell. Front legs are large with big scales and claws.

Color: Tan and brown body and shell, which blend into the desert environment.

Garter Snake
Size & Shape: Long, thin body with a small head. About 2 feet long.

Color: Dark green body with light yellow "ribbons" that run from the head to the end of its tail. (Some garter snakes also have red stripes and checkered patterns.)

Northern Leopard Frog
Size & Shape: Slightly larger than a mouse, or about 4 inches long. Bulging eyes and thick, strong limbs.

Color: Brown and green with dark spots over the body and limbs. Light ridges along the back.

Habitat & Behavior

Location, habitat, and season are clues that can help you make an educated guess as to what species you're seeing. If you're on the Pacific Coast or in southeastern parts of the United States, the frog you see is probably not a northern leopard frog. If you're in a lush meadow, you are probably not looking at a desert tortoise.

What is the animal doing? Is it resting in the sun or looking for food? How is the animal moving its body?

Is it making a noise, such as a croak or a chirp? Any other interesting characteristics?

Desert Tortoise

Habitat: Seen year-round in the deserts of the southwestern United States. Lives in burrows when temperatures are very hot or very cold.

Behavior: Moves slowly and eats vegetation in the desert scrub. Uses strong, sharp claws to dig burrows in the ground.

Northern Leopard Frog

Habitat: Lives in marshes, ponds, and wet meadows and grasslands. Present in the United States and Canada.

Behavior: Spends most of its time in or near water. Quick jumper. Hunts insects, worms, and smaller frogs.

Garter Snake

Habitat: Found throughout the continental United States, in Mexico, and in southern areas of Canada.

Behavior: Active during the day. In colder climates, it hibernates in the winter.

11

COMMON BOX TURTLE

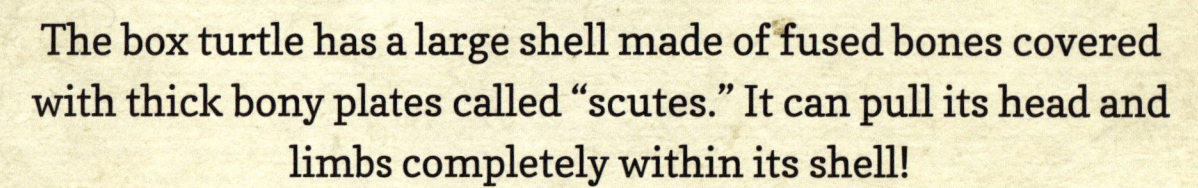

Terrapene carolina

The box turtle has a large shell made of fused bones covered with thick bony plates called "scutes." It can pull its head and limbs completely within its shell!

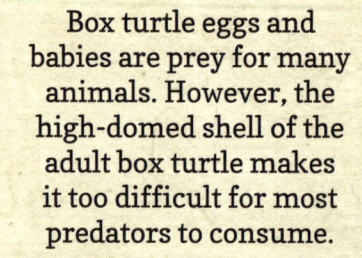

Box turtle eggs and babies are prey for many animals. However, the high-domed shell of the adult box turtle makes it too difficult for most predators to consume.

There are six *Terrapene carolina* subspecies, each with widely varying color patterns in the shells.

Order: Testudines
Family: Emydidae

Diet: Fungi, plants, berries, slugs, snails, and earthworms

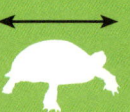

Size: 4 to 9 inches long

Habitat: On moist ground in open forests and along the edges of wetlands

Found throughout eastern North America

12

1

2

3

4

5

6

7

13

ALLIGATOR

Alligator mississippiensis

The alligator is a large reptile with four short limbs, a long snout, sharp teeth, tough skin, and a flat, powerful tail.

How do you tell the difference between a crocodile and an alligator? An alligator has a wider snout that hides most of its teeth when its mouth is closed.

The skin of an alligator's back contains hard, bony plates, which protect the alligator's organs from harm.

Order: Crocodylia
Family: Alligatoridae

Diet: Fish, small mammals, reptiles, amphibians, and birds

Size: 10 to 12 feet long, up to 1,000 pounds

Habitat: Freshwater rivers, lakes, swamps, and marshes

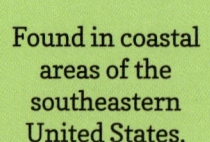

Found in coastal areas of the southeastern United States.

1
2
3
4
5
6

Keep far away from this animal! The alligator is a very dangerous predator. If you see one in the wild, view from a distance with an adult.

15

PACIFIC TREE FROG

Pseudacris regilla

This frog is green and brown and has large, bulging eyes. It has long digits and limbs that are great for climbing, but despite its name, it is usually found on the ground or in low vegetation.

The tree frog's skin ranges from light yellow-green to dark olive. Some frogs will slowly change colors and patterns when the seasons change, to help them blend in with their environments.

The body of a tree frog may be wet and slippery, but it has sticky pads on the ends of its toes to help it climb.

Order: Anura
Family: Hylidae

Diet: Insects

Size: Up to 2 inches long

Habitat: Forests, grasslands, and among plants around wetlands, such as marshes, wet woodlands, and ponds

Found in western areas of the United States

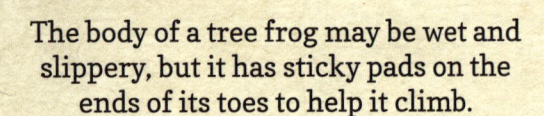

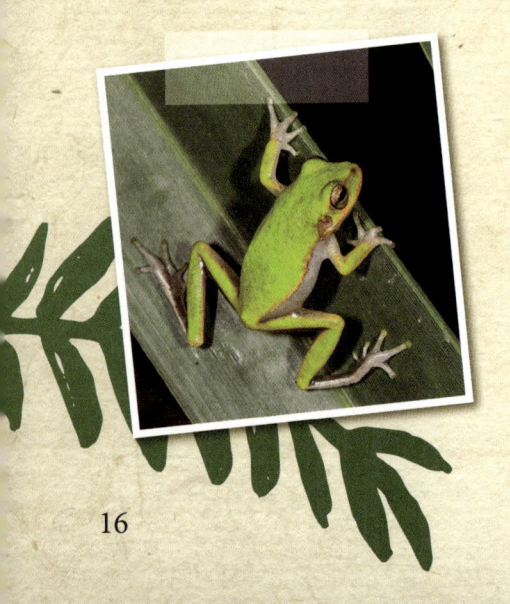

16

1

2

3

4

5

6

7

17

RED SALAMANDER

Pseudotriton ruber

This salamander has no lungs. It can be orange-brown to a bright red color, and the older it gets, the darker its spots become.

The red salamander is a nocturnal amphibian, which means most of its waking hours are at night. During the day, it can be found tucked away under rocks, logs, leaf litter, or other coverings.

The red salamander is one of the lungless salamanders. It absorbs oxygen from the air and water through its skin and the lining of its mouth.

Order: Caudata
Family: Plethodontidae

Diet: Insects, spiders, worms, and smaller salamanders

Size: 4 to 6 inches long

Habitat: Small streams and moist woodland environments. Both aquatic and terrestrial

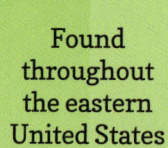

Found throughout the eastern United States

1

2

3

4

5

6

19

INCREDIBLE INSECTS

Entomology is the study of insects. When you're watching and recording information about these critters, you are a naturalist and an entomologist in training!

Leafcutter bee

Woolly bear caterpillar, which turns into the Isabella tiger moth

Known as the "mother of entomology," Maria Sibylla Merian (1647–1717) is famous for her discoveries regarding the butterfly's fascinating life cycle. She was also a skilled artist who created detailed drawings and paintings of the insects and plants she studied.

Insect Basics

What are insects?
Insects have six legs, two antennae, a body made up of three segments, and an exoskeleton (or a hard outer shell instead of internal bones and a spine). Many insects also have wings.

How many are there?
Insects make up the largest group of living organisms on the planet. There are about 1 million described species of insects, and scientists estimate that there are millions more not yet discovered!

What are the main groups of insects?
The four largest orders of animals under the class Insecta include Coleoptera (beetles), Diptera (flies), Lepidoptera (butterflies and moths), and Hymenoptera (ants, bees, and wasps). There are more than 360,000 beetle species on Earth—more than any other type of insect!

Monarch butterfly

Are they insects?
Is a spider an insect? No! A spider has eight legs, two body segments, and no antennae. Is a centipede an insect? No! A centipede has too many legs and body segments. Is a housefly an insect? Yes! It has wings, antennae, and three body segments.

IDENTIFYING INSECTS

Size

Compare an unfamiliar insect with one you know well. Is it bigger than a fly? Smaller than a butterfly? Low-to-the-ground like an ant?

Shape

What is the insect's overall shape? Does it have big, visible wings? Does it have compound eyes? Long legs?

Color

What are the insect's main colors? Are they bright to warn predators, or do they blend into the environment?

Blue Dasher Dragonfly
Size & Shape: About the size of a smaller moth, about 1.5 inches long. Long, skinny body tapers toward the "tail."

Color: Males are mostly blue. Females are yellow and brown.

Buffalo Treehopper
Size & Shape: Tall, thin body with a sharp point above the head.

Color: Mostly green to match the surrounding leaves.

Ladybug
Size & Shape: Small with a rounded body.

Color: A shiny red outer shell with black spots, a black head, and black legs.

Habitat & Behavior

Think about where you are, what kind of habitat you're in, and what season it is. For example, if you're hiking in the Rocky Mountains, the dragonfly you see is probably not a blue dasher. If there are no trees or bushes around, the insect you see is probably not a treehopper.

What is the insect doing? Is it in a tree or on the ground? Is it still or active? Does it fly, jump, or crawl?

Blue Dasher Dragonfly
Habitat: Found near still water, such as lakes, ponds, and marshes. Lives in Mexico, the United States, and southern parts of Canada; avoids dry, high-altitude areas, such as the Rocky Mountains.

Behavior: The male spends much of its time near the water's edge, whereas the female typically stays among vegetation.

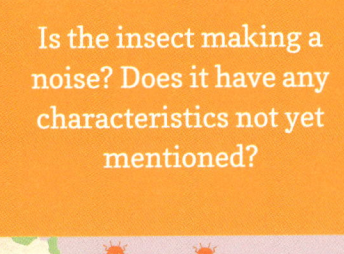

Is the insect making a noise? Does it have any characteristics not yet mentioned?

Treehopper
Habitat: Found in areas full of trees and bushes. Ranges from Mexico through the United States.

Behavior: Often appears very still like a leaf but hops or flies quickly when disturbed. Feeds on plant sap.

Ladybug
Habitat: Found in forests, grasslands, and gardens. Widely distributed in North America.

Behavior: Flies to find food (larvae, aphids, and other plant-eating insects). Also flies when disturbed.

23

MONARCH BUTTERFLY

Danaus plexippus

The monarch is known for its bright orange, black, and white coloring. This butterfly migrates every year and can travel thousands of miles!

The easy-to-spot monarch butterfly does not need to blend into its environment. Its bright appearance warns predators that it is poisonous and unpleasant in taste!

The monarch migrates south to Mexico for the winter. When spring arrives, a new generation flies north. Monarchs west of the Rocky Mountains migrate to the southern California coast for the winter.

Order: Lepidoptera
Family: Nymphalidae

Diet: Nectar; the caterpillar's host plant (where it lives and eats) is milkweed

Size: 3.5 to 4 inches wide

Habitat: Meadows, open fields, and gardens with milkweed

Found throughout the United States and in Mexico

24

1

2

3

4

5

25

CRICKET

Genus: Gryllus

The cricket has strong hind legs for jumping and is best known for its chirping sound. There are many species of different sizes, shapes, colors, and behaviors.

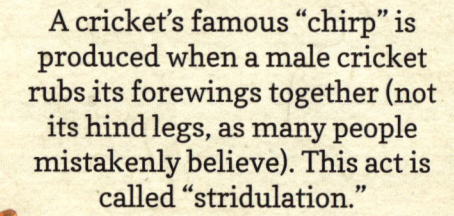

A cricket's famous "chirp" is produced when a male cricket rubs its forewings together (not its hind legs, as many people mistakenly believe). This act is called "stridulation."

Crickets chirp faster as the temperature increases.

Order: Orthoptera
Family: Gryllidae

Diet: Small insects, larvae, rotting plant matter, flowers, fruit, grasses, and seedlings

Size: 0.12 to 2 inches long

Habitat: A variety of environments, including fields, meadows, and wooded areas

Found throughout North America

1

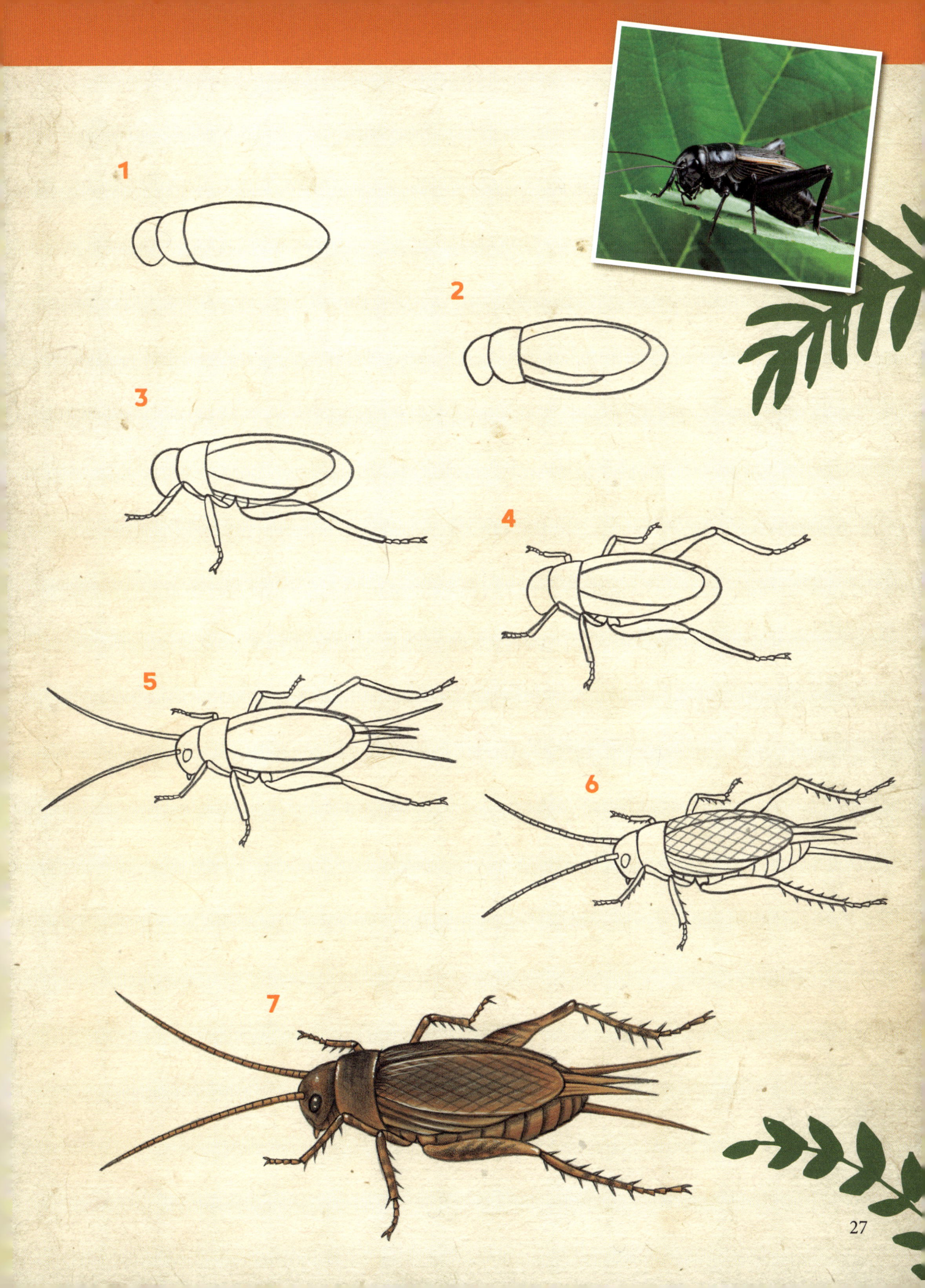

2

3

4

5

6

7

27

WALKING STICK

Diapheromera femorata

This slender insect disguises itself among plants and trees. Its coloring and spiny, ridged body provide excellent camouflage, making it look just like a stick!

The walking stick's eggs are also camouflaged. They look like seeds!

If a walking stick in its nymph stage is attacked and loses a leg, it can grow a new one. The new leg is often smaller than the original.

Order: Phasmida
Family: Diapheromeridae

Diet: Fresh leaves, especially from oak and hazelnut trees

Size: About 3 inches long

Habitat: Deciduous woods and forests

Found in the eastern United States and in southern Canada

1

2

3

4

5

29

YELLOW JACKET

Genus: Vespula

The yellow jacket wasp is a winged insect with a black-and-yellow coloring. There are several species of wasp grouped together as "yellow jackets."

While some people are afraid of the yellow jacket because it can sting repeatedly (unlike bees), this insect is actually very beneficial for humans. It eats many plant pests that kill crops of food that people eat.

Some wasps are solitary, but the yellow jacket lives in a colony and builds a nest underground. A colony can contain thousands of workers!

Order: Hymenoptera
Family: Vespidae

Diet: Insects, spiders, carrion, fruit, and nectar

Size: 0.5 to 1 inch long

Habitat: Lawns and the base of trees or shrubs

Found throughout North America

1
2
3
4
5
6
7

Yellow jackets usually won't bother you if you don't bother them or disturb their nests. However, they can sting repeatedly—and some people are severely allergic to their stings. Be very careful and keep your distance.

31

CONTINUE THE ADVENTURE!

Now that you've gotten to know some of North America's fascinating animals, don't stop learning! There are endless mammals, birds, reptiles, amphibians, and insects to seek and study. Besides looking in your own backyard, go to local parks and hiking trails. Make a list of all the nature preserves, animal sanctuaries, and national parks that you'd like to visit. You'll be surprised at how many resources await you!

Ladybug

About the National Wildlife Federation

Securing the future of wildlife through education and action since 1936, the National Wildlife Federation is one of America's largest conservation organizations. In January 1967, the National Wildlife Federation started publishing *Ranger Rick®* magazine, which has cultivated generations of young wildlife enthusiasts to become lifelong partners in protecting our environment alongside its charismatic ambassador, Ranger Rick, and his friends.

Read more Ranger Rick! Check out the *Ranger Rick*, *Ranger Rick Jr.*, and *Ranger Rick Cub* magazines at RangerRick.com.

And get these other guides from Ranger Rick:

Also available!

National Wildlife Federation Naturalist

David Mizejewski is a naturalist, author, and television host. As a wildlife expert, he appears on many television and radio shows, from *TODAY* to *NPR* and *Conan*, and is a Nat Geo WILD host. A lifelong nature lover, David spent his youth exploring woods, fields, and wetlands, observing and learning all about the natural world around us. He lives in Washington, DC.